It's Simple, Said Simon

W9-ADN-539

It's Simple, Said Simon

by Mary Ann Hoberman

illustrated by Meilo So

Dragonfly Books · New York

To Theo Moszynski, with much love—M.A.H.

To Joe and Brightness—M.S.

One day, Simon met a dog.

"I bet you can't growl," growled the dog.

Simon growled a low growl.

"Very good," said the dog.

"It's simple," said Simon.

Next, Simon met a cat.

"I bet you can't stretch," purred the cat.

Simon stretched a small stretch.

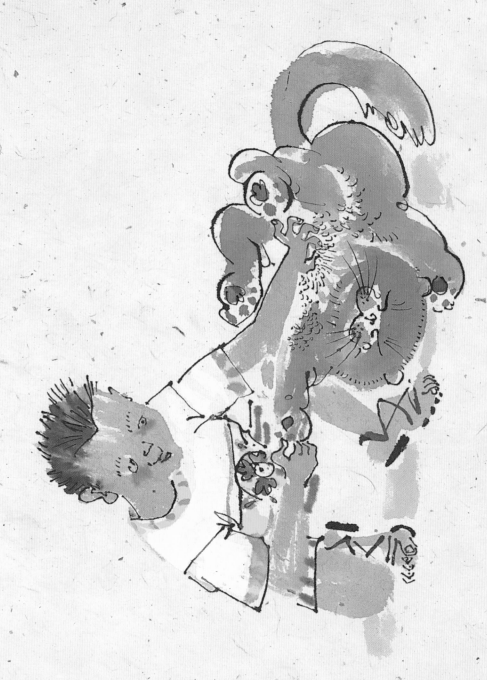

"Very good," said the cat.

"It's simple," said Simon.

Farther on, Simon met a horse.

"I bet you can't jump," neighed the horse.

Simon jumped a short jump.

"Very good," said the horse.
"It's simple," said Simon.

Then Simon met a tiger.

"I bet you can't growl," growled the tiger.

Simon growled a low growl.

"That's not loud enough," growled the tiger.

Simon growled a louder growl.

"Still not loud enough," growled the tiger.

GRRR GRRR GRRR

Simon growled a really loud growl.

"Very good," said the tiger.

"It's simple," said Simon.

"I bet you can't stretch," said the tiger.

Simon stretched a small stretch.
"That's not long enough," said the tiger.

Simon stretched a longer stretch.

"Still not long enough," said the tiger.

Simon stretched a really long stretch.

"Very good," said the tiger.
"It's simple," said Simon.
"I bet you can't jump," said the tiger.

Simon jumped a short jump.

"That's not high enough," said the tiger. **a higher jump.**

Simon jumped

"Still not high enough," said the tiger. **a really high jump.**

Simon jumped

"Very good," said the tiger.

"It's simple," said Simon.

"I bet you can't jump up on my back," said the tiger.

Simon jumped up on the tiger's back.

"Now I've got you," said the tiger, and off he trotted into the jungle.

It began to get dark.

"Could you please take me home now?" said Simon. "It's almost suppertime, and I'm hungry."

"I am, too," said the tiger.

"I'm having an egg for my supper," said Simon.
"I'm having a boy for mine," said the tiger.

"I'm thirsty," said Simon.

"I am, too," said the tiger, and he ambled down to the river.

"I can't reach the water," said Simon.
The tiger waded out a little.

"I still can't reach it," said Simon.
The tiger waded out a little farther.

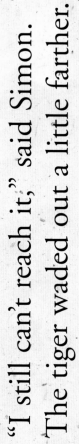

"I still can't quite reach it," said Simon.

The tiger waded out as far as he could.
Simon leaped off his back and began to swim.

"Help!" yelled the tiger.
"I can't swim!"

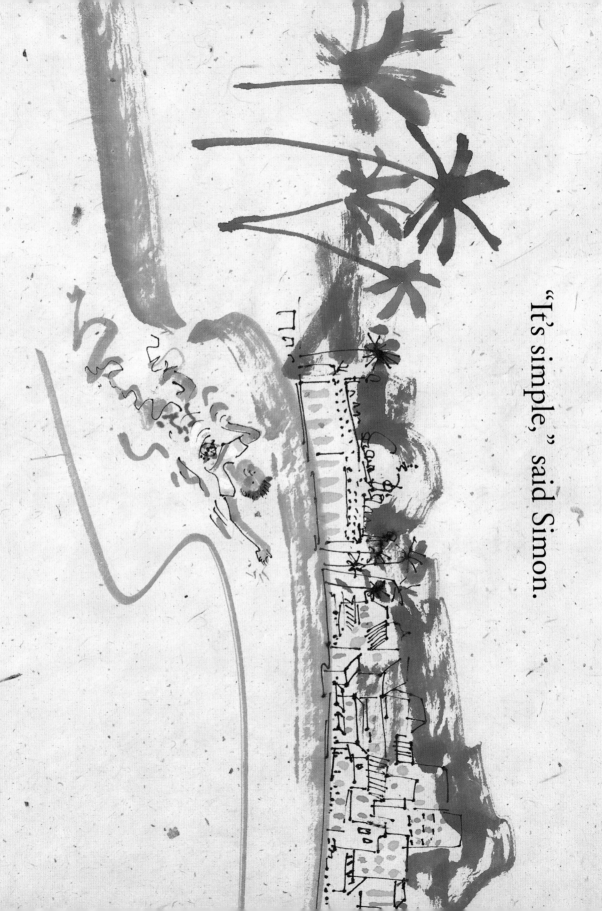

"It's simple," said Simon.

And he swam down the river and got home just in time for supper.

Visit us on the Web! www.randomhouse.com/kids

Educators and librarians, for a variety of teaching tools, visit us at
www.randomhouse.com/teachers

The Library of Congress has cataloged the hardcover edition of this work as follows:
Hoberman, Mary Ann.
"It's simple," said Simon / by Mary Ann Hoberman; illustrated by Meilo So.
p.   cm.
Summary: After successfully meeting the challenges posed by a dog, cat,
and horse, Simon meets a tiger that is much harder to satisfy and that he
must outwit before he becomes the tiger's dinner.
ISBN 978-0-375-81201-9 (hardcover) — ISBN 978-0-375-91201-6 (lib. bdg.)
[1. Tigers—Fiction. 2. Humorous stories.] I. So, Meilo, ill. II. Title.
PZ7.H6525 It 2001
[E]—dc21
0004283I

ISBN 978-0-440-41772-9 (pbk.)

MANUFACTURED IN CHINA

11 10 9 8 7 6 5 4 3 2